The Chain

by

Keith Gray

First published in 2006 in Great Britain by
Barrington Stoke Ltd
18 Walker Street, Edinburgh, EH3 7LP

www.barringtonstoke.co.uk

Reprinted 2009

ISBN: 978-1-84299-362-0

Printed in Great Britain by Bell & Bain Ltd

A Note from the Author

Most of the books I read when I was younger I got from the library. My problem was choosing my next book. There were so many to choose from. The shelves were packed. How did I know which one I'd enjoy most. To help me I came up with a plan.

I ignored the cover, and I didn't read the blurb on the back. Instead I looked on the library label inside to see how many people had borrowed the book before me. If there was a long list of black-stamped dates it meant loads of people had borrowed the book before me. So it must be good, right? Well, not always. Some people have <u>really</u> bad taste!

But I always wondered who those people were who had borrowed the book before me. Were they anything like me? Were they a boy or girl? Old or young? Had the book made them laugh or cry?

The Chain is about four people and one book. And it's about all of the different things a book can do. And all of the different reasons I think books are brilliant.

For Anna & Malcolm,
hoping the link between you is always
strong

Contents

Link 1: Cal's Test

Chapter 1

Mr Webster, the English teacher, was sitting back in his chair and reading the book. He didn't look up. He mumbled, "Shh. Quiet, please," even though no-one in the class had said a word. He pushed up his glasses and went on reading.

The class was hushed. The only sounds were the scribbling of pens and the rustle of paper. Everyone had their heads bent over their work. Everyone seemed to know just what to do. Everyone except Cal Brady.

He stared at the questions Mr Webster had written on the board and didn't know where to start. He watched everyone else working hard. Then he looked down at the blank piece of paper in front of him again. He began to worry.

His friend, Luke, was sitting next to him. Cal gave him a nudge.

But Luke took no notice.

Cal read the questions on the board again. But again they didn't make any sense at all. Cal was beginning to get that cold, fluttery feeling of panic in his belly.

The class was working on some horror stories by a writer called Edgar Allan Poe. Yesterday Mr Webster had told them to read one of the stories for homework. But Cal hadn't had time, and now all of the questions on the board were about that story. Cal enjoyed English and got good marks most of the time. He also liked horror stories.

Reading one of the stories for homework shouldn't have been a problem. Cal even liked Mr Webster. He was one of the younger, more interesting teachers. It made Cal feel even worse that he was letting Mr Webster down.

Should he tell Mr Webster he was stuck? But Cal didn't dare admit he hadn't done his homework.

He nudged Luke harder.

Luke frowned. He looked up. "What?" he whispered.

Cal checked to make sure Mr Webster wasn't watching. "Can I copy?"

Luke looked surprised at first. He made sure Mr Webster wasn't looking, then he pushed the paper with his answers towards the middle of the desk.

Cal quickly started to copy out Luke's answers.

"Make it a bit different to mine," Luke whispered.

Cal had never copied anyone's work before. He'd never had to. Normally it was the other way round. People asked if they could copy from *him*. This felt strange. But Cal wanted to change, didn't he? Wasn't this how he wanted to be? He'd better hurry up and get used to feeling like this.

At the end of the lesson everyone got up and went out. They left their work on Mr Webster's desk for him to mark. Cal wanted to get out of the classroom as quickly as he could but Mr Webster put down the book he'd been reading and looked up at him as he went past.

"What did you think?" Mr Webster asked with a smile. "Did you enjoy that story?"

Cal didn't know what to say. He felt bad and blushed. He could feel the hotness in his cheeks.

"Mmm. Yeah. It was OK," he mumbled.

Mr Webster pushed his glasses up again. He ran a hand through his thinning hair. Then he looked back at Cal as if he expected him to say something else. "I thought it would have been your kind of thing," he said. "Right up your street."

Cal was a rubbish liar. He just wanted to go, get out of there, get away. "It was good," he said. "I did like it."

Mr Webster stood up and put on the tatty blue jacket he always wore. "It was a little bit like the story you wrote for me last term, remember?"

Cal could remember the story he'd written, but there was no way he could know if it was anything like the one he should have read for homework last night. "A bit, maybe," he said softly.

Mr Webster stacked the class's work into a pile. He put Cal's work on top and tapped it with his finger. "Well, I'm looking forward to seeing what you thought of it anyway," he said. "I'm sure you'll have had some good ideas, you always do."

Cal shrugged, nodded, then went out quickly. He was glad to get away.

Chapter 2

Luke was waiting for him in the corridor. It was lunchtime and they walked together towards the dining hall.

"You OK?" Luke asked.

Cal just shrugged.

"I'm surprised," Luke said. "It's not like you to skip your homework."

"I didn't have time," Cal said. "I had other stuff to do."

"What like?"

Cal didn't answer at first.

"Come on," Luke said. "What other stuff?"

"I was out with Tully and them," Cal told him.

Now Luke was shocked *and* surprised. "Tully Harper? You were out with Tully Harper and his mates?"

Cal pulled a face. "Yeah. So?"

"But he's a nutter," Luke said. "Him and his gang are always in trouble."

"He's going to let me into the gang." Cal said it as if it was the smallest thing in the world.

But Luke didn't believe him. "*You*? I thought Tully used to beat you up all the time. Why would you want to hang around with him?"

"Because of what you just said." Cal copied Luke's voice like he'd copied his work.

8

"*It's not like you to skip your homework.* I'm fed up with what people always say about me. Why can't I be like Tully if I want to be?" He didn't say that he thought Tully might not bully him any more if he was one of their gang.

Luke shook his head. "You're mad," he said. "It sounds like a stupid idea to me." He went on and on about it. "You're nothing like Tully. You should always *get the better of* kids like that, never *join* them."

Cal took no notice. They put their bags in their lockers and were just about to join the dinner queue when Tully came up the corridor in front of them.

He was a tall kid, taller than some of the teachers, with spiky, black hair. He had a small silver ring in his right eyebrow but the teachers made him wear a plaster over it in school. He towered over Luke and Cal.

"Are you in a rush?" he asked Luke.

"No," Luke said.

But Tully nodded his head. "Well, you are now," he said. He pointed down the corridor away from the dining hall. "You need to get down there. Fast."

"Are you coming?" Luke asked Cal.

But it was Tully that said, "No, he's not."

And all Luke could do was leave Cal to it.

Cal tried not to look nervous. Tully had bullied him in the past, but not any more. Cal was going to be in Tully's gang. Luke just didn't understand because he'd never been Cal Brady. He'd never been top of the class all the time. And he'd never been bullied because of it.

Tully grinned at Cal. "Good last night, wasn't it?"

Cal nodded. "Yeah," he said but he didn't really agree. All they'd done was mooch around the park with Tully's dog. It was a huge, black monster of a thing called Boss. It did nothing but bark and snap.

"I've decided what your test's going to be," Tully told Cal.

"Test?" Cal was puzzled.

"If you want to hang around with me you've got to pass a test first. You've got to prove you're one of us."

Cal was worried. "What is it?"

"Who's your favourite teacher?" Tully asked.

"I don't know." Cal shrugged. "Maybe Mr Webster."

"Yeah, he'll do." Tully's grin grew even bigger, showing his teeth. "Your test is to steal something from him, something personal. Steal it and bring it to me tonight."

Cal didn't know what to say.

Tully grinned so hard he looked like his dog. "Easy as that. You do it, you're in." He was still grinning when he walked away.

But Cal was too nervous to smile back.

Chapter 3

Cal didn't want to do Tully's test. But he had to. It took the rest of the day for Cal to pluck up the courage to do what Tully had told him to.

When the bell went at the end of the day everyone grabbed their coats and bags and went off home. Except for Cal who was waiting in the toilets. He waited until the school was quiet and still. Then he sneaked along the silent corridor to the English room.

If Mr Webster was still there, Cal knew he wouldn't be able to steal anything. And part of him hoped Mr Webster *was* there. It wouldn't be his fault then, would it, if he couldn't steal anything? Tully would understand and maybe even let him off the test.

But when Cal looked in through the door's glass panel he saw that the English room was empty.

OK, he thought to himself. *Maybe the door's locked. I won't be able to steal anything then either. Tully will understand that too.*

But when Cal pushed down on the handle, the door swung open.

Cal waited. He didn't want to step inside the room. He chewed the inside of his cheek. It was now or never. He checked up and down the corridor to make sure no-one else was around. He had to do it. *Now*. His heart was thumping.

He darted into the room and up to Mr Webster's desk. There were papers and exercise books piled on top, a couple of pens, a bottle of Tippex. Tully wouldn't be happy with anything like that. The teacher's blue jacket was hanging on the back of the chair, but there was no way Cal going to steal that.

He was beginning to panic. What could he take? *Come on, come on*, he thought, *Mr Webster will be back any minute!* He nearly turned and ran out but he made himself stay.

He yanked on the desk's drawers but they were all locked. Maybe he should check the jacket's pockets? No. It would feel even worse to go through Mr Webster's private stuff. Worse than stealing. Then Cal spotted something at the edge of the desk under some papers. It was the book Mr Webster had been reading in class. Cal grabbed it and ran.

Chapter 4

As soon as he was off school ground and outside the gates, Cal felt better. He stopped running. He walked fast and didn't look back. Mr Webster's book was under his jumper against his chest. His heart beat hard against its cover.

Wow! He'd never done anything like this before. Never stolen anything. And he felt ... Well, he felt kind of light-headed and kind of excited. Because he'd got away with it, hadn't he? He hadn't been caught. He wanted the next few hours to go quickly so he could give the book to Tully and pass the test to be in his gang. From now on he'd never have to worry about being bullied.

He hurried home. His mind replayed over and over what he'd just done as if he was watching a chapter on a DVD. Cal told himself he didn't feel bad about stealing, he just felt good about getting away with it. He wasn't thinking about anything else, even when he went to cross the road. And the sudden blaring of a car horn shocked him.

He jumped back, out of the way. The car swerved, its wheels locked and screeched and it only just missed him. But then Cal saw the driver. He was wearing glasses.

Mr Webster!

Cal knew he'd been caught. He didn't know whether he should run or not. Mr Webster must have seen him take the book and then chased him. Everyone must be able to see the book. It made a huge lump under his coat. Anyone could see he was hiding something.

But when the driver poked his head out of the window to swear and shake his fist at Cal, Cal saw it wasn't his English teacher. Mr Webster had the same kind of glasses, but he didn't have much hair. This driver had a messy mop of red hair. In fact, he didn't look like Mr Webster at all.

Cal turned round and walked away fast. He felt shaken by what had just happened. Not only had he nearly been run over, but as well as that he'd really thought the driver was Mr Webster. He'd thought Mr Webster was chasing him. Cal headed home and tried not to think about it any more.

He turned the corner at the top of his street. Tully had said to meet up in the park at seven o'clock that evening. Cal wished seven o'clock would come quick so he could get rid of the book. He got to his house, pushed open the gate and walked up the path. His mum was in the front room, he could see her through the window. She waved but he couldn't wave back. He thought he must look a bit odd because he couldn't let go of the book.

But he almost dropped it when he saw a man in a blue jacket at the window next to his mum.

Mr Webster!

Cal couldn't move. His heart boomed. Mr Webster *did* know. He must have come straight round to Cal's house to see his parents. The book felt hot against Cal's chest. Hot enough to burn his skin. Cal felt so guilty and shocked he nearly dropped it.

Then Cal saw the man in the blue jacket wasn't Mr Webster. It was his dad. He blinked.

Cal felt even odder. It was as if he was going a little bit mad. He opened the front door and stepped in. His dad met him in the hall.

"What do you think of my new jacket?" his dad asked. "Your mum got it in the sales for me."

Cal looked at it. "Yeah. It's nice," he said. It was brand new, not old and tatty like Mr Webster's. Why had he thought his dad was Mr Webster?

"I got you some trousers, Cal," his mum shouted from the front room. "Do you want to try them on?"

"Later," Cal said and turned to go upstairs to his room.

He didn't stop when the phone rang. He let his dad answer it. Cal wanted to get to his room and get rid of the book. Hide it under his bed or something until tonight. Cal's guilt made the book feel even heavier.

He was half-way up the stairs when his dad called out, "It's for you, Cal. It's Mr Webster."

Chapter 5

Cal walked slowly, so slowly, back down the stairs. There was a horrible feeling of cold fear in his belly and the book felt as big as a brick against his chest. He wanted to say, "Tell him I'm out." But he didn't want either of his parents to talk to Mr Webster. He took the phone from his dad and went into the kitchen. He closed the door.

Cal held the phone for a few seconds and didn't say anything. Then, in a nervous voice, he said, "Hello?"

"Is that Cal Brady?" a voice said. It sounded put-on. "Have you been cheating on your tests, young man?"

Cal almost fell over with relief. "Luke? Luke, you dick-head! What do you think you're doing?"

Luke laughed loudly on the other end of the phone. "Just trying to freak you out."

"You're not funny, Luke," Cal said nastily. He put his hand to his forehead to wipe away the cold sweat.

"Please yourself," Luke said.

"What do you want?" Cal asked.

"I wanted to see if you were going to come round to my place tonight. My brother's got a couple of DVDs out and ..."

Cal cut him short. "I'm meeting Tully. I told you I was."

"I know," Luke said. "I just didn't think you were stupid enough to really do it."

"You could come too," Cal told him.

"No, thanks. I don't want anything to do with him or his gang of nutters," Luke said. "You can do what you want, just don't expect me to join in. Trust me – Tully's not worth the hassle. Just wait till you're in trouble with your mum and dad, the school, and the police too. Just wait till your new friends have all pissed off and left you. Then just come round to mine to have a laugh and watch some DVDs, OK?"

Luke put the phone down. Which was lucky because Cal didn't know what to say back.

Maybe Luke was right. Maybe if Cal got in with Tully he'd be in a lot of trouble. Cal wasn't even very good at being like Tully. All he'd done was nick a book and ever since he'd been scared of his own shadow.

He pressed the book against his chest through his jumper.

No, he thought. *I've already gone to all this trouble. I can't stop now.*

"I'm going out," he shouted to his parents and he headed back down the hall to the front door.

"Who was that on the phone?" his dad asked.

"Just Luke messing around," Cal said.

"What about your tea?" his mum shouted.

But Cal had already slammed the door on his way out.

He ran to the end of his road, then went left onto Lowman Street to the bus stop. It was only half past five. He knew he'd get to the park too early, but he hoped Tully or one of the others might arrive early too. All Cal wanted to do right now was get rid of the book.

It started to spit with rain. There were about six other people huddled in the bus shelter. Cal was sure they were all watching him and that they knew he had something hidden up his jumper. He tried to take no notice, but he could feel their eyes looking at him as if they were checking him out to inspect him. A young mum had her little boy in a pushchair and the toddler started to stare at Cal as if he had X-ray eyes. Cal turned his back on the kid and moved a few steps away, out into the rain. He wished the bus would hurry up.

Cars whizzed by on the road. Trucks, vans, motorbikes. But no bus. Cal paced up and down. He still held onto the book tight, up under his jumper. It rained harder. More people joined the queue. Cal was sure they were all watching him too. At one point he turned around to see the toddler in his pushchair still staring. So Cal pulled a face, which made the toddler cry. And then everyone really was looking at him. Cal crossed both his arms over his chest to try and help hide the book. His guilt and nerves were like hot butterflies in his belly. He hopped from foot to foot.

At last the bus arrived. Cal couldn't get onto it fast enough. He went straight up to the top deck because the mother and toddler stayed downstairs. He really wanted to sit at the back, but those seats were all taken, so he had to sit somewhere in the middle. When the bus lurched into motion he thought he could feel eyes burning into the back of his neck. He kept turning around to see if anyone was watching him.

"Calm down," he told himself. "No-one knows you. No-one knows what you've done. The book's hidden."

The trouble was it didn't feel hidden. To him, it felt as big and easy to see as if he had a slab of pavement stuck up under his jumper. But he'd soon be rid of it, that was the point. It would be Tully's problem soon, and Cal would be in his gang.

He thought about what Luke had said. Did he really want to be in Tully's gang? *"You should always get the better of kids like that, never join them,"* Luke had said. Maybe Cal should be looking for a way to get the better of Tully, instead of trying to be like him.

The bus pulled over at another stop. The windows on the top deck were misted-up and Cal rubbed the grey-wetness away with his fingers. He looked down at the queue of people waiting to get on ...

A man in a blue jacket ...

With not much hair ...

Cal swore loudly. He rubbed at the window with both hands trying to see more clearly through the wet smears. And as he put both hands up to the window, he let go of the book and it slid out from under his jumper. It bounced off the seat and landed on the floor with a thud.

Cal left it there. He jumped up and charged down the stairs. He almost tripped over his own feet. He pushed past the man in the blue jacket, the man he thought was Mr Webster. Of course, it wasn't him. This man was wearing a blue *anorak*, not a jacket. And he had a baseball cap on his head so Cal couldn't even see his hair. But Cal didn't care. He jumped off the bus before the doors shut.

The bus drove off with the book on its top deck. Cal stood in the rain and watched it go.

Good riddance, he thought.

He had a choice now. He could be out in the cold and rain at the park with Tully and his stupid, ugly dog, or he could be at his best friend's house having a laugh and watching a couple of DVDs. Cal reckoned it was an easy choice. He ran down the road towards Luke's. Maybe together they could come up with a way to get the better of Tully and his mates.

Link 2: Joe's Luck

Chapter 1

Joe's dad had once told him, "The less poker you play, the better off you'll be."

And Joe's dad knew just what he was talking about, because he always lost. But he'd taught Joe how to play poker anyway.

They used to play a lot when Joe was younger. They would bet Smarties instead of plastic cash chips. But they hadn't played for a long time now. Not since Joe had started to win. His dad didn't like losing to his 16-year-old son. And maybe that was because his dad still kept on losing to everyone else as well. His dad was a gambler. A bad one. His dad was a loser.

Joe didn't want to be like him. Joe didn't gamble. But tonight he had £100 in the back pocket of his jeans and he was going to play poker. The £100 was all that was left. It wasn't much. But his dad had lost everything else. Tonight Joe was going to win any way he could.

He'd heard about the poker game from some friends of his at college. A wannabe card-sharp student ran a game every Friday night. This guy was always on the look-out for new players. There was often big money, big bets. The players used their student loans and sometimes they had hand-outs from their rich parents. It was the money that interested Joe.

He waited in the rain for the bus. When it came at last, he paid the full fare and headed up to the top deck. He brushed the rain out of his hair as best he could and settled low in his seat. It was a half hour trip to the college campus. Joe wasn't too nervous. He was a sharp player. He reckoned he stood a good chance against stuck-up rich kids. His big worry was they might not let him join the game. Only then did he think about what might happen if he lost his £100.

The bus jogged along. It turned slowly at a roundabout and something slid out from under the seat. It was a book that someone must have dropped. He bent down to pick it up. He flipped through the pages. He didn't read any of it but it got him thinking.

His dad had once told him, "Poker isn't a game of chance. It's a game of skill. No matter how lucky you get, a skilful player will walk away with your cash every time."

Joe believed what his dad had said, but he didn't believe in relying on just luck or skill.

33

He flicked through the pages of the book as if it were a deck of cards, thinking, thinking.

Chapter 2

It was still raining when the bus arrived at the campus. It didn't take Joe long to find the blocks of student flats. At the main door was an electronic entry system with a long list of names by the buzzers. His friends had told Joe to look for Felix. That was the name second from the top.

When he pressed the buzzer, a voice came over the intercom. "Yeah. Who is it?"

"I'm here for the game," Joe said.

"Who are you?" the voice asked.

"My name's Joe, but you don't know me."

"So why should I let you play?"

"Because I've got a hundred quid in my back pocket," Joe said.

"Top floor," the voice said. The door was buzzed open.

Once he was on the top floor Joe could hear music and chatter coming from one of the student flats. He stepped into the flat and followed the music into a cramped, smoky room. There were movie posters and pictures of sexy women from the pages of *FHM* all over the walls. A few empty pizza boxes were pushed into a corner. In the middle of the room was a round table with four lads sitting at it. They all looked up as Joe came in.

They were all older than him and Joe knew they thought taking his money was going to be as easy as taking sweets off a baby. But he wasn't going to let that worry him. He gripped onto the book he'd found. He was looking forward to proving them wrong.

One of the lads was dressed so the whole world could see his expensive clothes labels, and he had long, blond hair that he fussed with as he spoke. His cigarette looked more chewed than smoked. "You must be 'Joe Who-I-Don't-Know'," he said, brushing his fringe out of his eyes. "I'm Felix. If you're here to play, then your money goes in the box."

There was a shoe box on top of the stereo full of cash.

Joe added his notes to the pile and counted out £100 worth of bright, plastic poker chips.

Felix grinned and raised his eyebrows. "Cool. Let's play some cards here!" he said.

Joe took the last empty seat. On one side of him was a guy wearing a suit and tie, and on the other, a fat kid eating crisps. Joe put his wet coat over the back of the chair. He still had the book in his hand and he put it on the table in front of him.

Felix tore the wrapping off a brand new deck of cards. He looked at Joe's book. "What's that you got there?" he asked.

"Found it on the bus," Joe said. "Thought it was lucky. Hoped it might bring me some more."

"Hope it didn't use all your luck up, more like," the fourth student said. Joe looked over at him. He was big like a rugby player and sat hunched forward over the little table. He wore tinted glasses that reflected the light.

The fat, crisp-munching student stopped eating for a few seconds to flip through the book's pages. He was pretending he was interested, but Joe knew he was really making sure there were no aces hidden inside.

Not yet, Joe thought.

Chapter 3

"Five card draw," Felix said. He was the starting dealer. After the first time all the players would take turns to deal.

Joe played carefully at first. He watched what the others did and tried to learn things about them. The more you knew about the other players, the better chance you had of winning their money.

The basic idea in poker is simple. When you think you have the best five cards, you try to get as much money into the pot as you can. You bet high to make the other players throw in lots of their money too. When your cards are lousy you fold, back down, and throw in your hand. You just have to wait until next time.

Or you can always bluff. You can pretend you've got good cards in your hand. But if you bluff, you'd better be a good liar. You just *have* to know who's bluffing and who isn't. You need to know which of the other players really do have better cards than you. You need to watch each one of them carefully.

Joe was good at watching. In the first few games he won some and he lost some. One time he had three 8s, another time, a pair of 3s *and* a pair of Queens. But he used the start of the game to watch the other players at the table.

The crisp-muncher next to him was easy to work out. Every time he had a good hand of cards, he said so.

"Would you look at these!" he'd shout through a mouthful of cheese and onion crumbs. "I'm raising you all! You can't beat this hand! You might as well just give me your money now!"

So, of course, nobody else raised the bets or added extra money to the pot for that game. And when the crisp-muncher won, all he got was loose change instead of big bucks.

They played more hands. Joe was doing OK. He scooped a big pot with a full house of 7s and Jacks, and was actually up by £48. But he didn't stop watching the others and trying to work them out.

The lad in the suit and tie was a sharper player than the crisp-muncher. He hardly said a word, but Joe soon found what he was looking for. Whenever the lad had good cards he would fiddle with his tie, as though he was nervous. It was a perfect "tell" for Joe to spot.

A "tell" is a little bit of give-away body language. People who are skilled poker players try to hide their own "tells". They try not to give off any signs that might let the other players know if they've got a good or a bad hand. At the same time, they do the best they can to work out what the other players' "tells" are. Working out a "tell" is like being able to spot if someone's lying. Every time Suit-and-Tie touched his tie, Joe knew the lad had good cards, so Joe folded and never lost any money to him.

That was why Joe always beat his dad. His dad's "tells" were written large in every move he made. Apart, perhaps, from the move he'd made this afternoon.

Back in the game and the big student opposite Joe had a tricky "tell" to spot. For a start, it was hard to look him in the eyes because of the light reflecting off his glasses. Joe lost three hands in a row to him. Then, at last, Joe worked out what his "tell" was.

The lad won a massive pot with rubbish cards and Joe noticed that whenever this student, Joe called him Glasses, had good cards, he put them face down on the table for everyone to see. But when he had bad cards and had to bluff, he held onto his cards tightly. Then he kept his cards close to his chest as if he thought someone might see how bad they really were. Now Joe knew his "tell", there was no way Glasses could beat him.

The game rolled on. The crisp-muncher was first to bust out and lose all his money. No-one missed him. He bet a lot of money with good cards and a lot of money with bad ones. It was no way to play. The others asked him to stay and deal but he walked off in a huff.

Joe was up to £165. Felix was in the lead with close to £200. No matter how closely Joe watched Felix, he just couldn't spot his "tell". Felix was one of the sharpest players Joe had come across. Joe had hoped to win without any tricks, but maybe he would have to give the luck of the cards, and his own skill, a bit of a helping hand.

He stared at the shoe box on top of the stereo, full of £10 and £20 notes. He wanted, *needed*, that cash.

Chapter 4

Joe had to wait a few more hands before he could make his move. Glasses was dealing and he dealt Joe an Ace of Clubs. Even with such a good card, when it was Joe's turn to bet he folded straight away. He threw his cards back into the middle of the table. But he didn't throw all five cards down, he kept one back – that Ace of Clubs. Joe prayed no-one would notice and he slid the Ace into the book on the table in front of him.

Glasses was too quick to scoop up the cards. He didn't notice the Ace was missing.

But the hidden card couldn't do Joe any good. For the next hour he lost nearly every hand. His stack of cash chips fell back to £105. The constant cigarette smoke was making his eyes sting and the whine of the music annoyed him. But he also hated cheating. He was feeling guilty and nervous. He couldn't keep his mind on the game.

"Come on, Joe-Who-I-Don't-Know," Felix mocked and pointed at him with his cigarette. "You losing your touch or what?" Felix went on to win a pot of £40 with only a pair of 6s.

Joe ran his thumb along the pages of the book. He was going to have to use that Ace soon. That was when Joe suddenly got it! He stared hard at Felix. Joe couldn't help grinning, and fought to hide it. He'd spotted Felix's "tell".

It was Felix's hair. He was always touching and stroking it. It didn't matter if his cards were good or bad, he was *always* playing with his hair. But Joe noticed that when Felix had a good hand, he preened, like a peacock. Then, when he had a bad hand, he pulled his fringe in front of his face and tugged on it as if he wanted to hide his eyes.

Once Joe knew this, he knew he could win. He didn't need to cheat.

Glasses bust out. He lost to Joe. Joe's stack of chips grew to £180. Half an hour later it had grown to £210. That was when Suit-and-Tie stopped playing. Felix and Joe were left to face each other off. Felix was winning. He had a stack of £290 in cash chips. Joe didn't worry. Once you know what someone's "tell" is, it's as if you can see their cards. It's as if you know something secret about them.

Joe didn't know what his own "tell" was. He hoped he didn't have one. When he played cards, he kept his face like stone and tried not to let anyone know what he was thinking.

His dad had said, "You're too cold for me, Joe. Stone cold."

Maybe that's why his dad had run out on them? Or maybe he was just a bad loser.

Joe slowly won back more and more cash chips. One time he bluffed and betted to win a massive £85 pot. That was when Felix began to turn nasty. He smoked more, called Joe names, swore at him. But Joe didn't let it get to him. He read Felix's "tells" and kept on winning the good hands.

At last Joe bust Felix out. And there in front of him was a stack of chips worth £500. Relief washed over him. He'd done it. He'd won. He gathered up the bundle of cash from the box on top of the stereo.

Felix turned to Glasses and hissed, "I told you we shouldn't have let him play. Look at him stuffing our money into his pockets." He glared at Joe. "You've got to let me try to win that back," he said.

Joe stood up. He picked up the book and put his coat on. "I've got to go," he said. "My mum'll worry if I'm late."

"Come on, Joe," Felix argued. He crushed his cigarette into the table top. "Be the man here. You've got to give me a chance. Double or nothing."

Joe shook his head. He wanted out. The smoky room felt too small, too close. But when he looked he saw Suit-and-Tie was blocking the door.

"I won fair and square," Joe said. "I just want to go."

"Double or nothing," Felix said in a hard, cold voice. He had a look in his eye that Joe knew very well. This kid was young and rich, but he had that nasty, greedy glint about him that Joe's dad got when he lost big time.

Glasses went to stand next to Suit-and Tie. Joe was trapped.

Chapter 5

Joe hated his dad. He'd come home from college today to find his mum in tears and his dad gone. His dad had taken all of their money, even the savings from the coffee tin in the kitchen cupboard. Joe hadn't seen the signs. His dad had kept the "tells" well hidden and had left them without anything to buy food or pay the rent. The only thing he left was a letter on the fridge door. It said he was being chased by men whom he owed money to. It was a letter full of fake apologies and at the bottom all it said was, "I.O.U."

The £100 Joe had come with tonight was all the money he had. He'd kept it hidden from his dad. He'd never trusted his dad with money. Joe needed the money he'd won tonight. It was the only hope for his mum and him.

"Double or nothing," Felix said. He didn't wait for Joe to answer. He shuffled the cards and slammed them down in the middle of the table. "We'll cut the deck now, instead of playing poker any more."

Joe wanted to play another hand of poker. Poker was skill. Felix wanted to just cut the deck of cards and see who got the highest. That was pure luck. It was gambling, plain and simple.

"Let me see your money first," Joe said.

Felix nodded at the other two students. They pulled out more notes until there was another £500 on the table.

Joe asked, "And if I win, you promise there'll be no more trouble? I can go?"

"*If* you win," Felix said with a sneer. He looked at his two friends. "Don't worry. I'll get all our money back now."

Joe tried to keep his face like stone, just the same as if he were playing any other hand. Felix fussed with his long hair. Glasses and Suit-and-Tie were silent, watching. Suit-and-Tie fiddled with his tie. The air felt thick. Joe was finding it hard to breathe. Felix bent forward and cut the deck of cards.

Felix showed the card to his friends first ... And they whooped! Glasses punched the air. Felix looked for himself. And only then showed it to Joe. King of Hearts. Felix sat back and laughed with his mates. They high-fived each other.

Yes, cutting the deck was gambling. But Joe hated gambling. Only idiots like his dad gambled.

And while the students were busy celebrating, Joe slipped the hidden card out from between the pages of the book. He kept it flat in his hand. Then he leaned forward quickly and cut the deck as if in a hurry. By the time the students were looking at him again, he was showing them the Ace of Clubs.

Chapter 6

Joe got out of the student flat and off the campus as fast as he could. Felix could change his mind any second and Joe didn't want to meet up with him or his mates again. Especially now, when his pockets were bulging with £1,000. He held onto the book tightly. He could hardly believe he'd got away with it.

It was after midnight and the bus had already gone, but he didn't mind the walk home. The rain had stopped at last. He was looking forward to giving his mum the money. He'd do it first thing in the morning. But he didn't want to tell her how he'd got it. He didn't want her to think he was turning out like his dad. He promised himself that would never happen.

He walked home along the high street past the shut-up shops. There was a second-hand bookshop about halfway down. Joe stopped for a while. He flicked through the pages of the book he'd found. The book that had helped him win.

Maybe it had been lucky after all.

He thought for a moment, then he pushed the book through the shop's letterbox. Whoever bought it might be someone else in need of some help. Maybe Joe could pass on a bit of good luck.

That was, *if* you believed in luck.

Link 3: Ben's Girlfriends

Chapter 1

"Do you love me?" Lisa asked.

Ben knew what she wanted to hear. "Yeah. Course I do." He kissed her quickly.

She gave him a huge smile. "I love you too," she said. "I'm so glad I met you."

He nodded. "Yeah. Me too."

They were coming out of the cinema after the early morning showing. It was a bright day, but chilly. Ben had thought the film had been rubbish, but Lisa had laughed right the way through. She'd been too busy laughing to do much else, even though she and Ben were sitting in the back row. Most of the time she'd sat very close to him and had not once let go of his hand. Even now she was hanging on as they walked down the busy high street. She was still smiling and laughing. Ben pulled her along. He was cold.

"Let's prove it to each other," Lisa said. "I want to prove we love each other."

Ben's ear pricked up. "What d'you mean?" Was this the moment he had been waiting for ...?

"Let's go and buy each other a present that shows how much we love each other," Lisa said. Ben could see she thought it was a wonderful idea.

Ben wasn't too sure. He'd been hoping she'd let him ... you know.

Lisa tugged on his hand. "Come on, it'll be fun," she said. She was excited now. "You go that way, I'm going this. We'll meet back at my house at two o'clock and swop presents." She smiled up at him through her long eyelashes. "My parents will be going out then."

"Oh, right," Ben said. "Right. OK."

Lisa gave him a long, slow kiss, then giggled. She ran back the way they'd walked. "Two o'clock!" she shouted to him.

Ben watched her go. *What on earth am I meant to do?* he thought.

He knew he didn't really love Lisa. They'd not even been together a month yet. He'd only said that to keep her happy. How was he meant to buy her a present that proved something he didn't feel?

They'd met at youth orchestra. Ben played the trumpet and Lisa played the violin.

Lisa had only joined a few weeks ago, but Ben had fancied her from the word go. She was tall, blonde and really pretty. She looked older than 15. She looked 18, easily.

Ben asked her out after only the second time she'd come to orchestra practice and they'd gone bowling together. They'd kissed for the first time on the bus going home.

She didn't let him do as much as some other girls, but maybe that would change today. If he could find the right present, everything might work out the way he wanted.

But he didn't know *how* to find the right present. He hated shopping anyway. It was a rubbish way to spend his Saturday.

There was a jeweller's at the bottom of the high street, but everything was too expensive. Ben had already paid for popcorn at the cinema. He didn't have much money left. He mooched around Woolworths looking at plants and ornaments and stuff. God! This was impossible. He looked at his watch. It was already ten past one.

He tried HMV, looking for love songs. A band he liked had a new CD, so he bought that for himself. But he had no idea what kind of music Lisa was into.

In the end, he went to the card shop on the corner near M&S. He'd have to find her something there. He was thinking he could just buy her a card and write a message about how much he loved her or something. In the window they had some little teddy-bears wearing T-shirts with messages printed on them. One was in a pink T-shirt that had a big heart on it and the words, "You're special". It cost more than Ben wanted to pay, but then if Lisa saw how much he'd paid, that would be a good thing, wouldn't it?

He bought the teddy and went to Lisa's house. He left the receipt in the bag.

Chapter 2

They were in her living room, sitting on the settee. Lisa had been right, her parents were out. Ben had tried to steer her upstairs to her bedroom but she wanted to do the present-thing.

She was excited. "You go first," she said bouncing up and down on the cushions. "No! I will! I will!"

Ben nodded. "OK."

"Close your eyes," Lisa told him. "And hold out your hands."

Ben did as she asked. He felt her put something flat into his hands.

"What is it?" he asked.

"Guess," she said.

He peeked at it.

"A book?"

Lisa clapped her hands in her excitement. "I was so pleased I found it. It was in the second-hand bookshop on the high street."

Ben did his best to hide how he felt. Fed up. He didn't read books. And this one was tatty. Its corners were bent as if it had been dropped lots of times. He pretended to flip through the pages and tried to look interested.

"It's my favourite book of all time," Lisa said. "It was just so brilliant the shop had it. And I wanted to share it with you. I love you so much I wanted you to have my favourite book of all time."

"Thanks," Ben said. He couldn't believe she'd bought him a second-hand book. How cheap was she? "It's ... nice."

"You'll love it. It's brilliant," Lisa gushed.

Ben simply nodded.

"Have you got a favourite book?" she asked.

"I have now," he replied.

Lisa laughed. "So what did you get me?"

He gave her the teddy-bear and was more than a little put-out that she didn't see how much it had cost him. He could tell she felt the same about her bear as he did about his book. If he'd known she liked that sort of thing, he'd have been happy to buy her a tatty old book.

At last, however, he got Lisa to take him upstairs. They didn't do much more than kiss, but he did manage to get her bra off.

Chapter 3

"I want to prove how much I love you," Ben said. He was with Kate now. His other girlfriend.

Kate shook her head. "We can't do anything. My mum's downstairs."

"No, not like that," Ben said. "I want to give you a present that proves I love you. Close your eyes and hold out your hands."

Kate looked surprised, but she did as he asked.

They were in her bedroom, sitting on the edge of her bed. Kate's mum was a bit more easy-going than Lisa's parents, but then Ben had been seeing Kate for four months now and her mum knew him better. Kate was more easy-going too. Even so, she and Ben had never gone all the way. Ben was hoping that tonight might be the night. He wasn't too happy with Lisa's book but it had given him an idea.

He took the book out from his coat and placed it in Kate's hands.

"Open your eyes," he said.

Kate was still surprised. "What's this?"

"It's my favourite book," Ben told her. "The best book I've ever read. And I wanted to share it with you, because of how much I love you."

Kate melted. Ben saw it happen. She took a quick breath, then let it out slowly as her eyes misted up. She held the book to her chest. She had a fantastic chest. She was a bit dumpier than Lisa. And she had brown hair when Ben liked blondes better. But she had massive boobs.

Sometimes when he was with Kate, Ben would feel bad about seeing Lisa behind her back. But then sometimes when he was with Lisa he thought he should break up with Kate. He never let himself think about it for too long. He knew Kate and Lisa would never meet because they went to different schools. They didn't even know each other.

"Thank you," Kate said. "It's such a beautiful thought. Thank you so much."

She put her hand to his cheek, then to the back of his neck and pulled him close to kiss him.

"You're wonderful," she told him. "I love you too."

Ben saw his chance and took it. He started gently pushing her backwards, down onto the bed. "Prove you love me," he whispered.

But Kate stopped him. "We can't," she said.

"Don't worry about your mum."

"It's not that," Kate said. "I'm going to see my dad in hospital. I promised I would."

"Yeah. Right," Ben nodded. "Sorry, I forgot." Kate's dad was really ill. Kate had told Ben what was wrong with her dad, but he'd forgotten that as well.

"Tomorrow night," Kate said.

"I can't, I've got orchestra practice. I can't get out of it because we've got a concert coming up."

"Soon, then," Kate told him. She kissed him. "I promise I'll prove how much I love you too. And I promise to read the book right away. It's so special."

Ben nodded. "I know." He really was very pleased with himself.

Chapter 4

The next day Ben met Lisa at orchestra. He told her how great the book was. In fact, all he'd done was look it up on Amazon and read some reviews. But she was pleased with what he said and that was the main thing.

"I've put your teddy on the shelf above my bed," she told him. "So it's the first thing I see in the morning, and the last thing I see at night."

"It's not *my* teddy," Ben said. "I had to buy it."

Orchestra went OK. To tell the truth, Ben was getting more and more fed up with having to go every week. If it wasn't for Lisa he might have quit already. The best part was always the walk home afterwards.

The orchestra had their practice in the school hall. Lisa and Ben always walked out of the hall hand in hand. It felt good to let the others know that they were a couple. But this evening Lisa was talking to the conductor. Ben went to wait for her outside the main entrance. He got the shock of his life when he saw Kate waiting for *him*. She was standing at the bottom of the stone steps on the footpath. He rushed over to her. He felt so glad he wasn't holding Lisa's hand tonight.

"What're you doing here?" he asked Kate sharply. He could see she was surprised by the way he asked.

"I thought it would be nice to meet you for once," she said. She was even more surprised when he ducked away from her kiss, but she tried not to let it show. "And I was desperate to thank you again for the book. I've been reading it."

She had it with her and showed it to him.

"I can see why you like it so much," she went on. "It's wonderful. I can't put it down. I was even reading it on the bus on the way here."

Ben kept checking the main entrance. What should he do? Could he get rid of Kate before Lisa came out? Or should he just walk away with her and leave Lisa behind?

"Are you OK?" Kate asked.

Ben thought he should get away fast and take Kate with him. He grabbed Kate's hand to drag her away.

But too late. There was Lisa. She came down the steps towards them carrying her violin case.

Ben dropped Kate's hand like it was on fire. In fact, he suddenly felt very hot all over.

"Hi," Lisa said to Kate.

"Hello," Kate said to Lisa.

They both turned to look at Ben. He racked his brains for something clever to say, or a good plan, or the world's biggest lie.

"Are you in the orchestra too?" Kate asked Lisa.

Lisa nodded. "Are you Ben's sister?"

Before Kate could answer he blurted, "Do you mind if I walk Lisa home, Kate? I do it most nights after orchestra. I'll call you tomorrow, OK? Is that OK?"

When Kate didn't reply, Ben turned to Lisa.

"Then again," he said, "seeing as Kate's come all this way, I think I should walk with her, don't you, Lisa? It's only fair."

How could he wriggle out of this one? He was telling himself it might be OK if he could get them away from each other.

Then Lisa spotted the book Kate had in her hands. "That book," she said, and pointed.

Kate smiled and held it up. "Have you read it? It's wonderful."

Lisa looked at Ben. Her pretty face creased into a frown as she tried to understand what was going on. "Is that the one I gave you?"

"It's a cold night," Ben said. "We'll freeze if we don't get going."

Kate said, "Ben gave it to me."

Lisa wasn't happy. "I gave you it because it was my favourite book."

Now Kate frowned too. "But that's why he gave it to me."

Lisa's face crumpled. She looked as if she was about to cry. "Did you give my book away to *her*?"

"Just a minute," Kate said, and she stepped up to the other girl. "Who are you anyway?"

"I'm Ben's girlfriend," Lisa said. Her voice was loud. It was almost a challenge.

Kate was gobsmacked. She looked at Ben, then at Lisa. Then back to Ben again. Her face had gone very white. "How long have you been cheating on me?" she asked him.

"Cheating?" Lisa squealed.

"On us both," Kate said.

"Look," Ben tried, "it's not what you think ..." But he didn't make it any further because Lisa suddenly smacked him on the back of the head with her violin case.

He didn't see it coming. He was knocked off his feet. He tumbled down the last few steps to the pavement. The grit bit into the palms of his hands and he cracked his elbow badly as he crash landed. The pain shot up his arm.

Lisa was sobbing. But that didn't stop her from swinging her violin case at him a second time, smacking him hard in the back. He yelped out at how much it hurt. He tried to say he was sorry but she was already running away.

Kate stood over him. "You shit!" she spat. "You total shit! I never want to see you again. Understand? *Never*!"

Ben was scared she was going to kick him in the balls or something so he curled up on the ground. She wasn't sobbing like Lisa, but her eyes sparkled with tears in the light of a street lamp.

"I'm sorry," Ben said. "I didn't mean—"

"Drop dead," Kate hissed. She almost flung the book at him. Then changed her mind and clutched it to her as she stormed off along the path.

Ben lay on the cold pavement staring up at the night sky. He couldn't believe how everything had gone so wrong. But Ben didn't blame himself. He blamed the book. It was all that stupid book's fault.

His elbow was stinging. And he had a painful lump on the back of his head from Lisa's violin case. What was he meant to do now?

"Are you OK?" said a soft voice from the top of the steps.

He looked back up the steps. It was Sarah who played the flute. She was standing there, by the main entrance. He'd always thought she was a bit shy. But very pretty.

"I tripped," he told her. "I think I might be hurt."

Sarah stepped slowly down towards him. "You poor thing. Can I help?"

Ben put on a brave face. "I think I might have broken something," he said.

Link 4: Kate's Courage

Chapter 1

Kate was sitting quietly at the side of her father's hospital bed. She didn't know what to say to him. She came to see him every day. He was her dad, but she never knew what to say to him these days.

He didn't look very much like her dad any more. He looked so fragile when he'd always been such a strong man. Tubes and wires came out of him like puppet's strings. She'd been told that the cancer was eating him up inside. The way she saw it, it was like the monster in the *Alien* movies. It was inside him, hurting him, like some horrible creature that would burst out of him any day soon. And when it did, it would kill him. Kate's dad was dying.

She sat with him in the still, small room and listened to the noises the hospital machines made. They were noises she'd only ever heard in the movies or on TV before and they added to the strange, almost unreal feeling in the room. Her dad was sleeping. Kate watched his paper-thin eyelids flutter.

She spent an hour or so alone with him every day. It was the time after the end of school and before her mother left work. Kate was never in a rush to get to the hospital. She walked there slowly from her school. And it made her feel guilty.

Her dad wasn't always awake. When he was he would ask her about school and what was happening in her life. Kate always mumbled her replies. Partly because she didn't know what to say, partly because she knew she might start crying at any second. And she knew he didn't want to see her cry. She wanted to be brave for him.

Why would he want to be bothered with her problems anyway? There was no way she was going to admit what an arsehole Ben had been to her. She'd get over him. She didn't need morons like him in her life right now.

As she thought about Ben, she remembered that she still had that book he'd given her. It was in her school bag. No matter what kind of a person Ben was, Kate had loved that book. She took it out now and flipped slowly through the pages.

Her father's soft voice made her jump. "Is it good?" he asked. He'd woken up and was watching her. "The book. Is it a good one?"

"Yes," Kate said. "Do you want to know what it's about?" She thought it would give her something to talk about.

"Why don't you read it to me?"

That was an even better idea. She smiled and turned to page one.

She read all the way up until the time her mother arrived at the hospital from work.

"You're right," her dad said. "It is good. Will you carry on for me tomorrow? I want to know what happens next."

Kate nodded quickly and gave a big smile. "Yes. Of course."

Chapter 2

And that's what she did. The next day, and the next. Every day while Kate was alone with her dad, before her mum arrived, she would read aloud to him while he lay and listened. He would often have his eyes shut but he promised he wasn't asleep and could hear every word.

Kate began to look forward to being with him now. She enjoyed that hour or so while she read to him. She started to hurry to the hospital from school. Her dad seemed as eager as she was to find out what happened next. He would say he was desperate for the next chapter and ask her to get settled and get reading!

Now and again a nurse might rush in to give her father an injection or check the machines. But Kate's dad just told her to keep reading. Maybe he really was enjoying the book as much as he said. Maybe it wasn't only to please her. They were sharing something, weren't they? Just the two of them. She had never felt so close to her father as she did when she was sitting reading to him.

After about a week, Kate could see they were getting near to the end of the book. She began to think about which book she would choose next. Could she find one they would both enjoy as much?

When she did at last come to the end of the book, she promised her father she'd be back with another one the next day. She had a choice of three or four, but she hadn't picked exactly which one yet.

But she never did get to read another book for him. Because that was the night he died.

Chapter 3

After the funeral her mum told her about what the nurses at the hospital had said. They'd all thought her dad would die sooner. They said they thought he'd hung on for those last few days because he wanted to know how the book was going to end.

Kate hoped that it was true. It would have felt much worse if he had died without knowing how the book ended.

The nurses also talked about how brave Kate had been when she had been reading to

him. But it hadn't felt like being brave at all.
She'd wanted to be there, with him.

"You should keep that book," her mother
said. "So you don't forget."

But Kate knew she would never forget.
And somehow it didn't feel right to keep the
book.

The next day she went for a walk and took
the book in her bag. She walked to the park
in the town centre. It was a beautiful sunny
day, but the world felt horribly lonely without
her dad. She sat in the shade of an old oak
tree, thinking about him and the book they'd
shared.

Kate thought about the book. She knew
that books could make you laugh, or make you
cry. They could be thrilling, or romantic, or
scare you. They could take you all around the
world, and beyond. They could make you see
things from someone else's point of view.
They could challenge you. They could help

you understand. They could bring comfort.
So much. So very much.

Kate thought books should be shared.

She took the book out of her bag and put
it beside her on the park bench. Then she
stood up and walked away. She left the book
there.

She turned to look at its cover and title
one last time as she went. She hoped
whoever read it next enjoyed it as much as
she had.

Barrington Stoke would like to thank all its readers for commenting on the manuscript before publication and in particular:

Alexandra Ackers

Daniel Bladon

Jamie Blakely

Charlotte Bowden

Michael Burns

Karin Carter

Tom Carter

Marion Critchley

Sally Farmer

Amanda Frame

Tasha Gadsby

Daniel Green

Louise Green

Deborah Hand

Jordan Hind

Daniel Holdsworth

Natalie Knutton

Chloe Lakin

Shirley Maddison

Hannah Markleew

Shona Owen

Jenny Rowlands

Amanda Yeoman

Mark Whalley

Become a Consultant!

Would you like to give us feedback on our titles before they are published? Contact us at the email address below – we'd love to hear from you!

info@barringtonstoke.co.uk
www.barringtonstoke.co.uk

Also by the same author

Ghosting

Nat and his sister help the living contact the dead. But this time the dead are talking back. And now the screams won't stop ...

Someone should have told them there are worse things than ghosts ...

You can order *Ghosting* directly from our website at
www.barringtonstoke.co.uk

Also by the same author ...

Before Night Falls

When Andy and his friends set out on a camping trip, they have no idea of the nightmare that lies ahead. Lucy vanishes then re-appears with strange bite marks on her neck. Can they uncover the dark secret of the moors – and make it out alive?

You can order *Before Night Falls* directly from our website at **www.barringtonstoke.co.uk**

Coming soon ...

The Return of Johnny Kemp

Dan got Johnny Kemp suspended from school, but now Johnny's back and he wants revenge! Teachers, friends and family can't help. Dan must face Johnny on his own ...

For more details please check our website at **www.barringtonstoke.co.uk**

If you liked this book,
why don't you try ...

Night Hunger

by Alan Gibbons

Ever since strange, sexy Beth sank her teeth into him, John's been feeling ... hungry. He craves meat, most of all at night. His hunger's leading him to a dark place, but can he stop himself, before it's too late?

You can order *Night Hunger* directly from our website at **www.barringtonstoke.co.uk**